ALWAYS

CARTER KIDS #1.5

CHLOE WALSH

Cover designed by JC Clarke
Edited by Aleesha Davis.
Proofread by: Brooke Bowen Hebert.

I would like to dedicate this book to my husband.
John, I love you more than life.
Thank you for my babies.
Thank you for your unequivocal love.
And thank you for being the beautiful person you are both inside and out.
You make breathing easy.
Always & Forever.
I promise.

AUTHOR'S NOTE

Always is the second book in the *Carter Kids* series.
It is a novella and sets up the premise to Hope and
Jordan's story, *Inevitable*. This novella is divided into
two parts: the past and the present.
Although it is not necessary, it is advisable to read
the *Broken Series* before reading the *Carter Kids*, as
many of the characters are in both series.
Due to its sexually-explicit content, scenes of abuse,
violence, and moderate bad language, *Always* is
recommended for mature readers of eighteen years
old and above.
Thank you for reading this.
Chloe. x

I

THE PAST

HOPE

Age 13

"If I told you a secret, would you keep it?"

We were sitting on the edge of the dock, with our feet in the water, and Jordan had his reading glasses on. I suspected he wore them because he had been crying, but I didn't want to embarrass him by saying so.

"I always keep your secrets, Jordan," I told him honestly. "You know that."

I'd been keeping his secrets since I could talk, and he'd been keeping his promises since as far back as I could remember.

"I hate it there, Keychain," he whispered. I knew exactly where *there* was, and it made the anger inside me boil to the surface. Three years ago, Jordan's mom, Karen, married this shifty-looking dude from her hometown in Idaho and moved back there, taking Jordan with her.

I'd never felt pain like I had the day Karen brought him to our house to say goodbye. I had known he was leaving, but I had been absolutely convinced – and so had Jordan – that Jordan's father, Derek, would step in and stop her from leaving. Derek didn't stop her and I lost my best friend that day.

I hated Derek for it, but my hatred paled in comparison to Jordan's.

Jordan made me a promise to me though: a promise to return – to always come back to me. And not once since the day he left had he broken that promise. Twice a year he came for me – not Uncle Derek – and spent the majority of his vacation at my house, and I loved him for it.

It wasn't easy for Jordan. Nothing in his life had been easy. I worried about him constantly, especially now, with that look in his eyes and that pain in his voice. He'd been home for summer vacation three days and I could tell he was different.

I wasn't stupid, I could tell something was … off … about his stepfather, Paul, and the whole damn situation, but I just didn't know what that something was.

I had suspicions, but no proof and I didn't like feeling useless. If I told my parents, my Dad would charge in like a protective lion, acting on his emotions, not logic; but Mom was much more clever. *She* would get to the bottom of Jordan's problem.

"Twenty-five days." Jordan glanced over at me, his green eyes damp. "And then I have to go back." He sighed heavily; his hand trembled next to mine, and I wasn't sure what to do to help him. "I don't want to go back there."

"You can come live with me." Shifting onto my knees, I turned to face him, the scuffed denim of my dungarees felt hot against my skin. It was so hot today. "I can talk to my mom," I told him. "She fixes everything. She'll talk to Dad, and he can stop them from making you go back. He can talk to your dad and tell him you're sad."

"I can't leave her there," he choked out. "As much as I don't want to go back there, I can't leave my mom."

I didn't know what to do; or how to help. I didn't care about Jordan's mom. I cared about him. I wanted him to be happy, and I wanted him here with me.

"Don't go back," I urged him. Something was happening to him in Idaho, and if he wasn't so insistent I keep his secrets, I could tell my mother about the bruises I saw on his body when we went swimming yesterday, or the way he flinched when he was touched. Jordan didn't like surprises and he cried in his sleep.

My mom would understand.

She would know what to do.

"If I asked you to do something for me, would you do it?" Jordan croaked, not meeting my eyes as he stared straight ahead. The only parts of our bodies that were touching were our fingertips.

He looked so nice, and smelled so good, and this weird tingling sensation came alive every time I touched his skin or sat close to him. When I was with Jordan, it felt like I was bursting with happiness and was on fire with excitement. At first, I was worried because I thought there was something seriously wrong with me, but then I decided I liked the feelings he brought to the surface. I liked him. My best friend. I had a crush on Jordan Porter.

"Anything," I vowed, covering his hand with mine.

I felt his hand tense underneath mine, but I didn't pull away.

"If I asked you to kiss me," Jordan whispered, "Would you do it?" Removing his glasses, Jordan shook his head and pinched the bridge of his nose with his free hand. "What I mean is: would you do it because you wanted to do it, or would you do it just to please me?"

I shook my head in confusion, as my stomach somersaulted around in my body. "What?"

"I need to know you'd say 'no', Hope," Jordan choked out, looking me in the eyes for the first time in what felt like forever. "I need that assurance." He squeezed my hand. "I need to know that you *could* say 'no'."

"I could never say 'no' to you, Jordy," I replied honestly. "Never."

"Please don't say that," he begged, dropping his head to stare at our hands. "Please."

"I'm sorry," I told him. Pulling my legs underneath me, I knelt, staring at the side of his face, waiting for him to turn.

He looked so incredibly troubled, and my heart broke to see him like this. He shouldn't have the worries I sensed he was carrying. He was only sixteen years old.

"Why are you so sad, Jordy?"

"Hope ..."

He paused and held his breath for a second, before letting out a sigh and climbing quickly to his feet. "Come on – enough of the sad talk! Let's go for a swim."

He dove into the water before I had a chance to call him out on avoiding my question.

Standing slowly, I placed my hands on my hips and watched as he swam to the surface. His black curls were clipped short and soaking wet.

"You coming, Keychain?" Jordan called out as he bobbed in the water, grinning up at me. He swam closer and splashed me with water.

"You better swim fast," I shouted back through fits of laughter, as I kicked off my ratty old tennis shoes and socks. "I'm gonna catch you, Jordan Porter."

"And I'm going to let you, Hope Carter," he said with a smile.

JORDAN

Age 16

He hit her again.

I was home three hours and that man had put his hands on my mother.

Hatred like I'd never known existed spewed through my veins, twisting my heart and forever blackening my stance on holy matrimony. But most of all, I hated myself.

I hated myself because I was hiding. My mom was inside that house getting beat on, and I was hiding in the barn, crying like a baby and wishing I were back in Thirteenth Street with Hope Carter.

"Get the hell out here, boy."

Clenching my eyes shut, I bit down on my fist

and held as still as I could, not daring to move a muscle. I was aching all over. I had tried to defend my mom earlier, but I was too fucking weak. Paul was bigger than any man I'd ever met in my life and my crushed nose was proof of his strength.

"Porter!"

I wondered if I held my breath long enough, remained completely still and didn't answer Paul when he called my name, would he forget I existed and leave me alone?

But then I thought of my mom and what he would do to her instead, and the fear began to spread like wildfire through my body.

My voice was tight as I crept out from under the bale of hay and said, "I'm here."

HOPE

Age 15

"That's completely unfair, Dad!"

I glared across the table at my father. Dad met my glare head on, with a look of anger of his own.

He was always my greatest opponent. Mom was soft – she caved easily – and the boys were stupid, but Dad: he was a warrior. This argument could go either way.

I hoped it went my way.

"Best friend's sleep over at each other's houses," I said in a level tone. "Do you want me to be friendless? Is that how you want to treat your only daughter?" I opened my eyes as wide as I could. "Your *favorite* child?"

"Eighteen-year-old boys don't sleep in fifteen-year-old girl's bedrooms," Dad countered quickly. His blue eyes were narrowed and focused on my face. "It's not happening, Hope. Get it out of your head."

"We're just friends, Dad," I growled, biting down hard on the inside of my cheek to keep my tongue in check. "And think very carefully about this," I added with a smirk, "I may be the only child you have who's prepared to care for you in your old age."

"I have four kids," Dad chuckled. "I figure I'll live with the youngest, and make the older three suffer."

"You'd prefer to live with Logan than me?" I asked in an appalled tone of voice.

"Logan doesn't threaten old age pensioners, Hope," Dad shot back with a grin.

"Let him stay, Kyle," Mom crooned, as she drifted into the kitchen, armed with a bucket full of cleaning detergents.

Mom had her dark hair pulled back off her face, and I had to hold in the gasp that tried to burst of me. As beautiful as my mother was - and she was gorgeous - the horrible scar she bore on her face still frightened me. She was scarred on every spare inch of her skin, but the one on her face was, by far, the worst one. It was so deep and distracting, but my dad never seemed to take any notice of it. He looked beyond Mom's scars.

I think I loved him a little more for that.

"He can sleep in one of the boy's rooms if you're worried, but he's a good boy. You know this."

I loved Mom even more for opening her mouth and sticking up for Jordan. Dad was a marshmallow when it came to my mother. The big, hotshot businessman in him fell to pieces when my petite mother came up against him.

"This is the last year, Hope," Dad grumbled, as he pushed his chair back and stood. "You're getting too old for this shit. It stops."

"Watch your mouth, Kyle," Mom warned.

"You like my mouth, Princess," Dad said with a smirk, as he prowled towards her.

And that's where I checked out.

Ugh.

JORDAN

Age 18

She was the most beautiful creature I had ever laid eyes on. I knew that sounded contrived, but never, in all my eighteen years, had I looked at someone so beautiful - so full of life.

I fed off Hope Carter's positivity, and I lived for her smiles. Being with Hope took the pain away; numbed the voices in my head; made me feel like I had a life worth living because I had her.

"You're staring again," Hope announced, stirring me from my reverie.

We were sitting at her parent's kitchen table. Hope was writing in her journal, and she was right. I was staring at her. Shaking my head, I buried the smile that was threatening to creep across my face and said, "Sorry."

"Don't apologize," she told me, flashing me one of those amazing smiles I craved. Brushing a dark curl back from her face, she rested her cheek in her hand and grinned. "I stare at you, too."

My heart slammed against my ribcage. It felt like it was trying to force its way out of my chest and into hers.

And then *his* voice penetrated my mind, and I remembered exactly why I didn't deserve the girl sitting opposite me.

"Say you like it, you little shit."

"I like it," I cried out, digging my fingernails into my flesh, piercing my skin, and wanting to burst into flames and disintegrate from this planet...

I was weak.

I couldn't defend my own mother.

I couldn't defend myself.

I didn't deserve shit ...

The feeling of suffocation built inside me at a rapid pace, causing my heart to palpitate and my palms to sweat.

"What's wrong?" Hope asked me, ever perceptive. Reaching across the table, she covered my large hand with her small one. "Talk to me, Jordan," she urged, entwining her fingers with mine.

My throat felt like sandpaper, and I couldn't get my words out, but I clung to her hand, savored the feel of her skin on mine like it was the last time I would ever get the chance. Hope was too young and pure to ever understand my life. But that's exactly what I loved most about her. She was untouched by the shitty things in the world – she was innocent and *good.*

Kyle Carter had made sure of that – her father had protected her from the bad things in the world. Like my father should have done for me – like he should have done for my mother …

"Did he do it again?" she asked me then, and I felt like dying.

"Do what?" I replied, desperately trying to hide my secrets and protect her from my truth. "What are you talking about?"

"Paul," she hissed, and her eyes flared with anger. Slamming her pen on the table, Hope roughly shoved her chair back and moved towards me.

I sat with my heart in my mouth, watching as she dropped to her knees in front of me. Gently, Hope reached forward and raised my T-shirt.

"This," she whispered, with tears in her eyes. Her

other hand snaked out; her fingers traced the yellow bruising on my side. "This," she repeated. A heart-breaking sound tore from her throat, and I couldn't take any more.

Dropping my hand to hers, I moved her hand aside and covered my stomach. "It's not as bad as it used to be," I choked out, desperately trying to reassure her. "I promise; it's not. I'm taller than him now. He can't get the better of me so easily …"

Shaking her head, Hope let out a harsh cry and lunged forward, burying her face in my lap. "I can't bear it," she sobbed. "I hate him."

"Me, too," I admitted, as I stroked her hair, blinking back the tears. "Me, too, Keychain."

HOPE

Age 16

I was in love.

I was head over heels in love with the boy sitting on my bed and the best part of it was I think he loved me, too. I couldn't be sure of course –well, I was sure he loved me as a friend, but did he love me as a girl? I wasn't so sure.

Jordan had always been careful around me, made sure we kept our relationship clean. He had realized long before I had that people would talk if we were too close.

I thought that was bullshit.

Jordan Porter was mine. He always had been, but

I knew what my sixteen years to his nineteen looked like to the outside world.

It looked weird.

They wouldn't see that we had been together from infancy, that he was the boy who had spent his life taking care of me, bandaging my cut knees when I fell out of our tree house or lost my balance on the monkey bars.

Jordan was the one who had helped me climb back up, and taught me to ride my bike. He was the one who had stuck up for me against my brothers and punched Billy Hobbs in the stomach for pushing me on the soccer field – he hadn't needed to do that since I rearranged Billy's testicles later that day – but the outside world wouldn't see the kindness in Jordan's heart, or the respectful way he held only my hand when we were alone. I mean he hadn't even kissed me, but all they would see – all my father would see – was a young man and a teenage girl.

Our age gap assured it.

"What do I mean to you?" I blurted out, never one to mince words. My cheeks reddened, I could feel them burn, but I kept my eyes on his face.

"Everything," Jordan replied immediately, never taking his eyes off the pad he was sketching on.

His fingers moved so fast across the paper – so

skillfully. I stared at him, drinking him in. He looked good: too good for the twin bed in my room he was sitting on. Too good not to touch.

And I was itching to touch him.

His hair was a mess - a sexy mess of curls - and his whole body was entirely too tempting. God, hormones had officially found me. This was only day three of summer vacation. We had at least another month together.

How the heck was I going to cope?

"Everything." I tested the word around, and decided that was a great answer. "You really mean that?"

"Of course," he added, with a chuckle. "You're my little Keychain."

I crawled over to where he was sitting, and climbed onto his lap, wrapping my arms around him. His whole frame tensed, and I felt pretty bad because I knew I'd just squashed whatever it was he was sketching.

"Hope?" Jordan said softly. Pushing me back gently, he glanced at my face. He must have seen something in my eyes, nerves or something, because he lifted me off his lap and sat forward. Now he was the one who looked wary. "What are you doing?"

"Do you have feelings for me, Jordan?" I asked.

"Like the way a guy feels for his girlfriend feelings?" Inhaling a deep breath, I decided to bite the bullet. "I hope you do, because I'm kind of in love with you."

There. It was out there. Now came the waiting part. "Actually, I'm a lot ..." I added, "I'm a lot in love with you."

"Hope ... I ... I should go," Jordan choked, as he jerked off my bed and moved towards the door. "You're too young. I shouldn't ... Your dad's right. I'm too old to be hanging out with you."

"You're nineteen," I shot back. "Not ninety. Age is just a number, Jordan."

"You're a kid," he said in a weary tone. "I'm sorry, Hope, but it's wrong."

My heart broke. Yeah, I was only sixteen, but I was pretty sure if someone took an x-ray of my chest at this moment they would see the split and the splintered pieces swimming around in my ribcage.

"Do you have a girlfriend in Idaho or something?" I asked calmly, following him out of my bedroom and down the hall.

He stopped outside the door of the upstairs bathroom, but I didn't.

Marching towards him, I backed him up against the door and pressed myself against him. He was a good foot taller than me, but I didn't care about that.

I was sick and tired of threading over this conversation. I needed to know where I stood.

"Is that it? Do you want someone else?"

"What?" He looked appalled. "No, I don't have a girlfriend, Hope, what are you talking about?"

Shaking his head, he murmured, "I only want …" He stopped abruptly, and then let out a heavy sigh. "I've only ever wanted you."

I didn't give him a chance to say anything else and ruin the moment. Instead, I grabbed him by the shirt and dragged his mouth down to mine. "Say it," I demanded. "Claim me."

"I love you," Jordan whispered, as he tucked a curl behind my ear and pressed a kiss to my nose. "I claim you. You remind me of what I need in my life."

"So what do you need in your life?"

"Hope." He smiled. "I need you."

JORDAN

Age 19

"Do you have a girlfriend in Idaho or something?" Hope demanded, as she stalked down the hallway after me. Pressing her slim body to mine, she looked into my eyes and asked, "Is that it? Do you want someone else?"

"What?" I shook my head, stunned by her question and bluntness. "No, I don't have a girlfriend, what are you talking about?" How could she even think that? "I only want ..."

I stopped and contemplated lying to her.

I didn't deserve her.

I knew I didn't.

I couldn't protect her like a real man could, but I couldn't lie to her either.

"I've only ever wanted you," I admitted in a torn voice, full of self-loathing.

What Hope did next caused an electric current so strong to ricochet through my body, turning me into a puddle of mush at her feet.

Grabbing my shirt she dragged my mouth down to hers and said, "Say it. Claim me."

"I love you," I admitted. With shaking hands, I tucked a curl behind her ear and pressed a kiss to her cute button nose. "I claim you."

HOPE

Age 17

"Are you going to tell me what's wrong?" I asked,
holding my breath, fearing his answer, hoping he
would lie and tell me he was fine, because that look
in his eyes was petrifying me. I had hoped things
would be different this year – better – but the
sadness in Jordan's eyes proved me wrong.

He was hurting.

I could feel it in the way his hands trembled. I
could see it in his eyes.

Something was wrong.

"Jordan," I whispered, when he didn't answer.

He didn't look at me.

Instead, he stared downwards. God, I knew this

conversation was going to end badly, and if I was my best friend, Ash, I'd know a number of different tricks to take his mind off his problems, but he wouldn't let me touch him.

God knows I'd tried...

"Hope, I don't ..."

He broke off and rubbed his face with his hand. "Just sit with me," he choked out.

Edging closer, Jordan bowed his head, rested his knee against mine and shuddered violently.

"This is all I can manage," he admitted. "Please don't ask me why."

"I won't," I told him, forcing myself not to throw my arms around him. I never asked and I never touched. He would freak out if I did, and I needed him close to me. I needed the smell of him in my nostrils, the weight of his knee against mine.

Besides, I had a pretty good idea of why Jordan didn't like being touched, and it had everything to do with his bastard stepfather using him as a punching bag.

"I love you, Jordan," I whispered, hoping to God and every angel, star, and whatever the hell was up in the sky that he would open up to me – that today would be the day he would tell me his troubles – the full extent of what had been happening.

"I'm never going to be the right guy for you, Hope," he husked, twisting his head to look at me.

His green eyes penetrated me, burned me.

"You'll figure that out soon enough, but it would be a hell of a lot easier if you would let me go now. Your dad's right about me."

"Don't," I warned. I was so sick of this conversation. I wasn't giving him up, not for Dad, not for Uncle Derek, not for anyone. He was mine and that was that. No one was going to take him away from me. *He* wasn't going to take *him* away from me. Jordan had this screwed up notion that he wasn't good enough for me. It was a bullshit notion and I wasn't letting him bring it up again ...

"Hope, I'm a train wreck," Jordan hissed. Leaning forward, he shook his head and sighed heavily. "I can't have a normal relationship with you. I can't be a normal fucking boyfriend to you. You deserve normal. Can't you see we're going nowhere fast?"

"You *are* a normal boyfriend," I assured him quietly. "You're just respectful. There's nothing wrong with that."

"You really think that?" he asked me in a desperate tone. "You have no doubts about me, no questions about my behavior?"

Loads ...

"I'm sure about you, Jordy," I whispered. The only parts of our bodies that were touching were our fingertips; they were the only parts Jordan would allow to touch. *Nothing new there...*

His eyes were so laden down with pain that my heart squeezed in my chest. His shoulders were shaking, so I carefully placed my hands on them to stop his trembling, and hoping he could feel what I felt. I edged closer to him until our faces were only a hair's breath from each other. "I love you," I told him again. "Always."

He closed his eyes and inhaled a ragged breath. "I love you, too." He was breathing hard and fast. His hot breath fanned my face, and I slowly closed the gap, pressing my lips to his softly. I curled my arms around his neck and climbed onto his lap.

He didn't touch me, didn't make a move or reciprocate my touch, but his lips kissed me back. He kissed me desperately, deeply, his tongue dueling with mine, setting alight every nerve in my body.

I moaned and wiggled in his lap, desperate to ease the aching inside of me – the aching only he roused. I may have been a virgin, but I wasn't naive and knew the pulsing in my clit was aimed, directed, and caused by the gorgeous man whose lap I was filling, and whose body I was feeling.

His heart was hammering furiously against his ribcage, and I couldn't stop myself from sliding my hand up his shirt to feel his hot, tight, muscled skin.

Mine ...

I was so thankful for him – to his mother – for creating this creature who seemed to have been put on this earth for the sole purpose of being my mate. My other half. I knew it was true. There would never be anyone else for me. This man was *the* man.

My man ...

"Touch me," I begged between kisses, as I sucked on his lower lip, pulling it into my mouth, sinking my teeth gently into his full, lush lip. "I want you to," I added, grinding myself on his lap, feeling his hardness. Knowing I was turning him on only egged me on further. "I want you – to be with you – properly …"

"Not until you're eighteen," he said quickly, as he drew his hand up and cupped my face. Disappointment flared inside me when he placed his other hand on my shoulder and pushed me back. "I won't touch you until then."

"I want this," I growled.

"You're not ready," he shot back, in an eerily calm tone of voice.

"Jordan," I said with a scowl. "I want to have sex with you. It's really not a big deal."

He glared at me. "See, you saying those words right there prove that you're not ready, Hope."

He let out a sigh and captured my hand in his.

Bringing my hand to his mouth, he placed a soft kiss on each one of my knuckles. "When you're eighteen," he whispered. "Not until then."

"Promise me," I demanded and Jordan froze.

I knew I had him then – he never broke his promises – so I pushed on.

"Promise me you'll be my first." I stretched back and studied his reddened face. "Promise me I'll be *your* first?"

I knew this was a pretty ballsy thing to ask a twenty-year-old man, but I didn't care. I demanded faithfulness. I deserved fidelity. I had offered Jordan my body – he had refused – so he could just wait for me.

Jordan's eyes burned with sincerity when he said, "I promise you the only firsts I'll ever take will be yours." He pressed a kiss to my forehead and sighed.

"And yeah, Hope," he rasped, "whatever I have – whatever you want to take from me – it's yours."

JORDAN

Age 20

I didn't think Hope would ever truly realize just how hard it was for me to stop earlier tonight.

She thought I didn't want her – like that was even fucking possible!

No, Hope didn't need to worry about whether or not I lusted after her. Even now, with her curled up in my arms on her parents' couch, my moral fiber was fighting a war – and barely winning – against my raging dick.

She felt so soft, tender, and so damn perfect that it was hard to breathe, because the emotions that girl evoked inside of me were smothering me.

Spending this time with Hope made all of the

sacrifices I had made completely worth it. But having her in my arms also made me feel completely unworthy. She had her life on pause for me. She was missing out on normal teenage activities because of me. Because I was either too old or too damn chicken-shit to partake in them ...

"Promise me something," she mumbled drowsily, tucking closer to my body.

"Anything," I replied without a second thought, tightening my hold on her pajama-covered waist.

"Promise me that I can keep you forever."

"Of course," I told her sincerely. She never needed to worry about that. I'd been born hers. Sometimes I wondered if I'd been put on this earth for her solely – because I sure as hell began and ended with her.

"Jordan, how long have you been loving me?"

I smiled at her question. "Constantly and consistently since I was four years old."

Hope had this vulnerability about her that very few people got to see. *I was one of those few people.*

"Next year ..." Yawning loudly, Hope stretched her body and turned her face to look up at me. Her big blue eyes locked on my face causing a tremor of pleasure to roll through my body. "I want to start my life with you. Properly."

"What do you mean?"

Cupping my cheek with her small hand, Hope brushed her thumb against my bottom lip and smiled.

"Our own apartment," she told me, her voice full of emotion, and my heart flipped around in my chest.

"Sex."

Her smile widened into a full megawatt grin and her voice turned playful.

"Engagement rings ..."

My smile mirrored hers when I said, "You want to marry me?"

"Are you asking me?" she shot back, grinning.

HOPE

Age 18

The majority of my classmates were counting down the hours until school was over and winter break began.

I was counting down the minutes until I saw him again.

I hadn't seen Jordan in over six months and I was growing antsy. I never had much patience, a trait I'd inherited from my hotheaded father, and waiting for class to be over was driving me insane.

Seven, six, five, four, three, two, one ...

Tonight I would be reunited with my best friend, the other half of me – the better part of me. I was eighteen now: legally an adult. Jordan had no more excuses to hide behind and I had no more patience.

Yeah, the boy who'd given me his word he would come for me was the reason I couldn't stop smiling. Seriously, it was like someone had shoved a clothes hanger in my mouth.

My jaw was aching, but still I grinned.

Twisting a lock of my hair around my finger, I sighed softly and continued my vigilant staring, all the while planning all the possible things we would do. The only word that kept popping into my mind was 'sex'.

It was like I had a neon sign flashing the word in my mind, until I began to shift uncomfortably on my chair, forcing my slut of a vagina to calm down and stop pulsing.

Calling my vagina – or any other part of my anatomy besides my vast imagination – a slut was a slight exaggeration since I was still a virgin.

Not for long, though.

Not after tonight.

I had no idea where we would go. Not his dad's house. Definitely not mine, but God, I couldn't wait to be with him. I felt like I had been waiting forever.

I *had* been waiting forever.

Jordan Porter – the boy – now man – I had spent

seventeen years of my life obsessing about – was finally coming home.

Permanently.

He had enough of Paul Smith's rules and bullshit and he was moving back to The Hill. Of course, my parents, and his, had no clue of this. They though he was coming home for winter break, but Jordan and I had plans – big ones I didn't have any intention of telling them.

Maybe when we got settled in an apartment and had every piece of furniture jammed against the door; maybe then I would tell Dad about my plans.

But for now, I would just bob and weave around his questions. Dad didn't need the stress and Mom didn't need the worry. But I wasn't backing down. I would walk over hot coals first. I was going to have what I wanted and my heart wanted Jordan. It was pretty simple in my mind.

No one was going to stop me …

"You look like a dope, Carter," my friend, Ash – aka Ashlynn Brooks – who was sitting beside me chuckled as she nudged me in the shoulder. "He's coming tonight?"

"He will," I smirked, flashing her a shit-eating grin. "A lot."

"Lucky bitch." Ash poked her tongue out and

pulled a face, before fiddling with her calculator, her long black hair brushed against my forearm as she studied the screen intently. After a few minutes she pushed to it towards me and I had to stifle a laugh. She had managed to write *"Sex"* on the screen.

"I'm sick with jealousy right now," Ash admitted without shame, and I couldn't blame her. Most of my friends were jealous of me. Not of me, no, it was more to do with my hot-as-hell boyfriend. My hot-as-hell boyfriend who rode a hot-as-hell Ducati; whose body was sinfully sexy, inked with my name; whose face was painfully gorgeous; and whose heart was one hundred percent mine.

Yep, I was pretty sure I was jealous of myself.

"All I'm doing this Christmas is spending time with my grandparents. All you'll be doing is *him*," she complained. "Which means you won't be at home and I won't have an excuse to stop by and ogle those sexy triplets."

"Ashlynn," I snapped, appalled at the thought of my best friend's intentions towards my baby brothers Cameron, Colton and Logan. "They're barely seventeen." *And they'd eat you up for breakfast and spit you out without a second thought ...*

"So?" Ash shrugged nonchalantly. "I could definitely turn cougar for one of those mini-versions of your dad." She smirked at me. "How is Mr. Carter?"

Ugh ...

"Do you mind?" I forced the bile that had risen in my throat back down and cast a warning glare at my so-called BFF. "How would you like it if I talked about your father the way you do mine?"

"Quite frankly, I'd be surprised," Ash shot back, her brown eyes twinkling with humor. "Considering my father is in his late fifties and is packing the pounds." She smiled dreamily. "You have no idea of how lucky you are, Hope," she added thoughtfully. "He's forty – *forty* –and he looks like he walked off a freaking runway. Not a gray hair in sight ... and those eyes."

"*These* eyes?" I bulged my eyes to make a point and glared at her. "And he's forty-one," I growled in irritation.

This drove me crazy.

It was seriously sick.

This was the reason I was careful when making friends of the female kind. They were so much worse than men. I felt I had the experience to make such a bold statement having lived with four testosterone-fueled, hot-tempered, egotistical men for all of my life.

My dad and my triplet brothers were the reason I'd spent so much of my life being wary. I couldn't count the amount of times I'd been tricked into friendship by a girl who just wanted to sizzle in on my family, and that wasn't an exaggeration.

My father had money – lots of it – and he was – I begrudgingly had to admit – a handsome man. He was also notorious amongst many of my friends' moms.

Yep, Dad was a little slutty in his day.

Thank God my mother had come along when she had, and straightened his ass out, otherwise God only knows whose womb my little seed would have been implanted in ...

Even though she teased me about the male members of my family, I knew Ash wasn't serious.

Well, she *was* serious, but not enough to jeopardize our friendship. And my other best friend, Teagan Connolly, was so wrapped up in Noah Messina I doubted she had even looked twice at my brothers.

Come to think about it ...

"Have you seen Teagan today?" I asked Ash.

Ash rolled her eyes to the heavens and let out a sigh. "That girl is a walking hormone." Shaking her head, Ash folded her arms across her chest. "Her and

Noah need to screw it out before they both burst into flames."

"Ashlynn," I chuckled.

"I'm serious," Ash shot back with a smile. "They do."

JORDAN

Age 21

My body was running on adrenalin.

I was pumped the hell up.

"Merry Christmas, asshole," I snarled before pummeling my fist into my stepfather's face for the final time. Groaning in agony, he collapsed on the bedroom floor before curling into a ball – his attempt at protecting his worthless ass.

"I'm not staying here," I told my mother breathlessly, as I clenched and unclenched my throbbing fists. "I mean it this time."

Staring down at Paul's injured carcass, I inhaled a calming breath and forced myself not to continue beating the shit out of the man who had taken everything from me. I took comfort in the knowledge that I had fought back. Now he knew he couldn't hurt me.

Never again.

Nodding her head slowly, Mom sobbed quietly, using the back of her hand to wipe the tears from her cheeks. "I understand," she murmured, as she wrapped a blanket around her bruised body.

"I'm going back to Colorado," I added, forcing myself to keep my eyes locked on my mother's heartbroken face. "And I'm not coming back here, Mom – I can't."

Mom's face contorted in pain, but she nodded, "I know."

"You can come with me," I croaked out, feeling helpless and fucking tortured. I wanted to stay and protect my mother from her piece-of-shit husband – that's why I had given up my scholarship to USC and enrolled in the community college – but I couldn't take anymore. "Dad can help you ..."

"No," my mother gasped, lowering herself to the ground to kneel beside the man who had fucking destroyed us. "I have to stay."

"Mom," I begged. "Please."

"Just go," my mother whispered, not meeting my eye. "Leave us, Jordan."

HOPE

Age 18

"Do you ever sleep?" Teagan growled in her thick Irish accent from where she was camped out on my bedroom floor. "Seriously, Hope, turn it off."

"Shh," I mumbled, eyes locked on the screen of my laptop. "One more episode."

I couldn't turn it off. Earlier tonight, Teagan had introduced me to this Irish television show called *Love/Hate* and I was completely hooked.

They men on the show were sexy and keeping my mind off worrying about why Jordan was late ...

"I need a drink," Teagan whispered, so I waved her off, mumbling "*Help yourself.*"

I continued watching my program until a very

loud – and very familiar – voice penetrated my eardrums.

"Yes, we're working things out, Derek. So if could you please fuck off and let us work things out it would be much appreciated."

Derek ...

"Jordan!" I squealed, knocking my laptop sideways in my rush to climb off my bed. I raced down the stairs two steps at a time, not stopping until I was in the lounge with my arms wrapped around my curly-haired boyfriend.

"Merry Christmas, Keychain," Jordan whispered against my neck as he knotted his hand in my curls. "I told you I'd make it."

"No way," Colton's familiar voice chuckled, followed by Cam's booming voice as he cheered, "I knew he was bagging her."

"Goddammit, Noah," I screamed when I noticed my brother's friend screwing some girl on our couch. "I can't believe you brought a girl into my ... Oh. My. God ..."

My words trailed off when I realized who Noah was screwing.

"Teagan?" I squeaked. "What are you doing underneath Noah ... and *naked*!"

"Nah," Colt chuckled. "I can see lace panties."

"Pervert," I shot back quickly.

"Hi, Hope," Teagan mumbled, twiddling the tips of her fingers that were wrapped around Noah's neck seconds before burying her face against Noah's chest.

"Hate to break up the family reunion," Noah said with his whole attention on my blonde best friend. "But could you guys take this into the kitchen so we can get up and out of your hair?"

"Yeah. Everyone go back to bed," I heard my dad order seconds before he appeared in the doorway, looking more pissed than usual. "Now!"

HOPE

Age 18

"I have something to tell you," Jordan whispered, folding me into his arms as we lay in the dark, staring up at his bedroom ceiling in his dad's house. "I'm going back."

"Why?" I managed to choke out. Jordan had been home two months. He had just enrolled in USC. He couldn't just leave school now. "You can't go back there – what about your classes?" *And me?* "You promised …"

"I know," he said, kissing my cheek. "But I can't leave her there."

Yes, you can …

"But you can leave me," I mumbled.

"That's not fair, Keychain."

"No, it's not," I grumbled. "It's not fair, Jordan. Nothing's been fair around here in a very long time."

"I'm sorry," he replied.

"Don't go back and you'll have nothing to be sorry for," I snapped.

"You don't know what he ..." His arm tightened around me.

"He's a bastard, Hope," Jordan admitted quietly. "My mother's husband is a fucking butcher, and I'm afraid that if I don't go back and get her out of there, the next time I'll see her will be in a coffin."

"Then tell your father." I sat up quickly at stared at his beautiful face. "Let him figure this out ..."

"Like he'd give a shit," Jordan spat, as he reached over me and switched on the lamp. "Besides, it's none of his business. Mom texted me before you came over – said she's leaving him. Permanently."

He shrugged. "She's my mother, Hope. I have to help her."

"And Derek's your father, Jordan. He could help ..." I began to say, but he interrupted me.

"This is *his* fault, Hope. He got her pregnant with me. He fucked off to college. He dumped her. He chased her right into Paul's arms. He's the reason I ..." Jerking off the bed, Jordan stormed over to his dresser and pulled out a sweater. "I tolerate Derek so I can be near you," he hissed. "That's it, that's why, and that's all it will ever be."

"He loves you," I said sadly.

"Not enough," was all Jordan replied in a tight tone of voice.

"Jordan …"

"Don't defend him to me, Hope," he snapped. Pinching the bridge of his nose, Jordan closed his eyes for a couple of seconds. "I'm sorry," he whispered. "I shouldn't have raised my voice to you."

I chuckled. "Jordan, that wasn't raising your voice. Believe me. I live in a house with four men."

"So when do you leave?" I asked after a while.

"Later tonight – after I take you home."

"That soon?" I swallowed the lump in my throat.

"I'm not giving her time to change her mind, baby," he husked. "This is huge. She wants out and I'm getting her out."

"I'm going to miss you." I forced myself not to cry. "How do I know you won't run off with some girl from Idaho while you're gone?"

"Because you own me," he replied immediately and my heart slammed in my chest. "Hope Carter, I've been yours since I could comprehend what you were, or how significant you would be to my life."

"So you're saying I'm important to you?"

"I'm telling you, you're everything to me," he whispered, before adding, "I'll be back in a few days – a week tops."

"I want some collateral," I teased. "You know; something that will bring you back to me."

"I'm always coming back for you," he rasped, and I couldn't hold back a second longer.

I lunged forward and pressed my mouth to his.

"What are you doing?" Jordan husked against my mouth, as I shoved him down on his bed and straddled him.

"I need you," I breathed, struggling to keep my breath even as I ground my body against his. "I'm done with waiting," I told him as I yanked his shirt out from his jeans. "I'm ready," I moaned.

Rolling off Jordan, I quickly stood and shoved my jeans off before lowering myself onto his lap once more.

"Slow down." Jordan held my shoulders in a firm grip as he craned his neck away from me. "Hope, slow down. We don't have to do this tonight." His pupils were dilated so much I could hardly see the green of his eyes, but still he held me back. "We don't have to do this tonight," he repeated slowly, his voice painfully torn.

Ignoring his rebuke, I lunged forward and thrust my tongue into his mouth. The pained growl that tore from his chest as I did so assured me he wanted me, so why was he trying to stop this?

He wasn't.

I wouldn't let him.

Covering his hand with mine, I slid it from my shoulder, directing it downwards; forcing him to cup my breast, to squeeze my flesh. To take what I was offering him.

My nipples were hard, puckered tight in antici-pation, and when he moved his other hand to rest on my waistline, and then under my shirt, I could have cried in victory. Rocking against him, I rubbed myself against him, getting off on the feel of him. "Take my top off."

"No," he replied, and it was immediate and final. His hands dropped away from my body limply. He glared at me. "Hope, we need to stop. Now!"

"You stop," I countered, ripping at his belt, freeing the button and fly on his jeans. "Stop refusing me."

Sitting up straight, I dragged my shirt over my head and tossed it on the floor. Ignoring his protests, I unclasped my bra and let it fall away from my body. Reaching out with my left hand, I grabbed his and entwined our fingers. "This is us now," I breathed. "No more waiting."

"I'm trying to protect you from making a rash decision ..." His voice trailed off as his eyes fell to my bare chest. Jordan swallowed deeply, causing his Adams apple to bob in his throat. He clenched his hands into fists, rested them on his thighs as he shifted uncomfortably.

I knew why.

The huge bulge in his jeans was the proof of his discomfort.

I took advantage of his attention and reached up to cup my own breasts.

"If you want to protect me, take out your wallet," I said huskily. "That's the only kind of protection I'm interested in from you."

I waited, eyes locked on his face, watching for any signs of his retreat. He let out a sharp sigh, leaned forward and hoisted me onto his lap, roughly capturing one of my nipples between his teeth. His free hand fondled my other breast.

"If we do this," he husked as his tongue lapped at my breast, "there's no going back. This seals it, baby."

"I know," I moaned, rocking my hips towards him, pushing my breasts into his face. "I can't wait."

Jordan let out a growl and grabbed my hips. "Lift up."

I did and dropping his hands to my hips, he slid my panties down my thighs, before lifting his hips and pushing his jeans and boxers down, freeing his erection.

And there it was: the cause of most arguments in my home.

Jordan Porter's dick.

I had to compose myself, fight down the rush of nerves and questions inside of me that were demanding to know how that thing would ever possibly fit inside me.

Jesus …

Grabbing his wallet, I watched in amusement and horror as Jordan tore open a condom wrapper and rolled it on, pinching the tip as he sheathed his erection.

My mouth must have been hanging open, because when I finally tore my eyes away from his face, Jordan was staring at me with an expression I didn't recognize. "Put your clothes on, Hope," he said softly. "You're not ready."

Panic filled me and without thinking I lowered myself onto his erection and made the biggest idiot of myself I ever could. I had been right.

It didn't fit.

It hurt, it stung like a motherfucker and he made no move to assist me.

Jordan grunted softly and lifted me off him and set me down on the bed next to him. I reached for his duvet and wrapped it around myself quickly, mentally counting down from ten in a bid to keep calm and not run out of the room howling like a wolf.

What a freaking disaster...

So much for magical first times.

I wondered if that counted since he technically didn't penetrate me. Oh Jesus, what if I didn't work right? What if he really didn't fit? What if *nothing* did? Dammit, I was seriously regretting not taking Ash's advice and using that stupid vibrator she'd bought me as a joke for my birthday.

I buried my face in the duvet and debated holding my breath. If I could pass out then I wouldn't have to deal with the mortification.

I had just made a complete ass of myself.

Oh, my God.

"Are you okay?" I felt an arm slip around my shoulders and then the side of my face was pressed against his chest. Jordan's heart was beating furiously in his chest. His skin was hot and moist. "Look at me, Hope."

I didn't.

I couldn't.

I was too freaking embarrassed.

"Ugh," I groaned. "Can we forget that I just molested you against your will and broke my vagina while doing it?"

He stiffened for a moment before chuckling softly and I died a little more inside.

Oh, great!

He was laughing at me.

Perfect.

Fucking fantastic.

"You're so dramatic."

"You're so … not," I muttered with a pout. "And I'm being serious," I added with a huff. "I think I broke a bone. Do you think there's a clinic that specializes in x-raying your womb?"

Jordan laughed, truly laughed, and it was a beautiful sound.

"God, I love you," he said as he rolled me onto my back and leaned over me, his elbows resting on either side of my face.

His eyes were locked on mine, piercing through

me like flashes of dazzling emerald. "I do, Hope," he whispered, rubbing my nose with his before lowering his lips to mine. He kissed me, deeply, passionately and my legs fell open of their own accord.

My heart leapt in my chest, my vagina fluttered, letting me know there was life in the old girl still. I wrapped my arms around his neck and let nature take its course.

And when he did move in me, push through me, it wasn't so bad. It was good, actually. Really good and I was ready.

Jordan trembled above me; his weight on my chest was heaven and my whole body ignited in an achy burning heat. Spasms of white-hot pleasure shot through my core as Jordan slowly moved inside me. "Are you okay?" he whispered, burying his head in my neck.

I nodded, biting down hard on my lip, as I arched upwards, my body chasing something I wasn't quite sure of, but knew I'd do just about anything to reach it. "Are you?"

"You feel ..." he shuddered, "I ... you're everything to me." He picked up speed, gently at first, and then he moved faster, harder, and rougher inside of me and I loved every second of it.

The soft moans coming from my throat became louder and louder until I was screaming in ecstasy.

Jordan seemed to thrive on my screams; as he circled himself inside of me, his thumb found my clitoris, and that's when I went a little crazy.

He growled.

I moaned.

He hissed.

I cried out.

His lips parted, his body spasmed and I ...

"What the hell are you doing?" a voice roared, breaking through the silence of our heavy breathing, tearing my good nerves to pieces.

The shame ... the pure, raw undiluted shame ...

Jordan's father stood in the bedroom doorway with his mouth hanging open.

"Get out of here, Dad," Jordan hissed.

Oh. My. God.

Jordan shielded my body with his, which didn't help much since his naked ass was sticking up in the air. I did the only thing I could think of. I grabbed the closest object on Jordan's nightstand and threw it at him.

It just so happened to be an apple.

"His daughter? Really, Jordan – my best friend's baby girl?" I heard Derek moan and I clenched my eyes shut. "Couldn't you have picked a girl who is less likely to have a homicidal father?"

"I love her," Jordan replied calmly. "I always have. That's not changing."

"He's going to kill you," Derek rambled. "He's going kill *me* – I've got to talk to Lee about this."

"Mom's getting a divorce," Jordan announced, and Derek froze on the spot. "I have to go back," he added. "Tonight – she needs me to help her with some … things."

"Do you …" Derek's voice caught in his throat and he seemed to struggle for a moment before letting out a shuddering sigh. "… you want me to come with you?" he finally asked in a voice thick with emotion. "Is she okay?"

"No," Jordan replied coldly. "But she will be. I'll take care of her. I've talked to Uncle Danny and he and Cindy will put her up for as long as she needs."

"Fine." Shaking his head, Derek turned for the bedroom door and said, "Put your clothes on Hopey-bear. I'll drop you home."

Ugh … "Okay, Uncle Derek," I said with a wince.

When Derek left the room, Jordan cupped my cheek and rubbed my nose with his. "I'll come back for you," he whispered. "I promise."

Age 21

My life had been a complicated tornado of events, emotions and mixed signals.

Sound pathetic?

Perhaps it did, but that didn't change the truth, and maybe I was pathetic.

I had my own definition of the word.

Pathetic was being fourteen-years-old and repeatedly having to watch your mother being beaten by the animal who, less than a week before-hand, vowed before God to honor and cherish her.

What a crock of shit.

Pathetic was my father who, after eighteen years, *still* preferred to keep company with a ghost.

Pathetic was me.

For not defending myself – for allowing the things that were done to me happen without a goddamn fight.

Pathetic was a twenty-one year old man who couldn't stop ...

No!

Clenching my eyes shut, I balled my hands into fists and forced the images and memories from my mind.

Block it out!

My goal in life was simple now: get as far away from Colorado and Idaho as I could. I wasn't picky, any place would do, but I had one small problem.

I had to tell Hope Carter I wasn't taking her with me.

Hope had been the very essence of my being for twenty-one years and, to be brutally honest, I didn't have a clue how I was going to get over her, but I knew I couldn't be with her.

I had sent her a text message on the drive up to Colorado saying I needed space, but even then I knew that wasn't enough. Hope wouldn't let me go without a fight, but I sure as hell needed her to because the thought of her ever finding out about me caused me physical fucking pain – worse than anything that bastard had caused ...

"Jordan, I really don't think this is a good idea," Dad muttered as we pulled up outside the red-bricked two-story house on Thirteenth Street. His jaw was tensed, his face set in a deep frown.

I really couldn't care less about what my father thought was a good idea or bad.

It didn't matter to me anymore.

None of it did.

"You're going to break her heart," Dad continued, oblivious to my lack of interest. "Kyle knows something is up, Jordan. I had to *lie* to him," he hissed. "I told him I caught you two making out last week and that's why I'm so upset, but he's not stupid."

Kyle could kiss my ass.

They all could.

Besides, after today, Kyle Carter wouldn't have to worry about me.

I was letting her go.

They had all gotten what they wanted. I was stepping out of Hope's life. She was better off without me anyway. She had a future ahead of her: a bright future, a loving family, and a stable home life.

I realized that now.

Hope Carter was going places. The girl I loved

more than life itself was going to shine like the star she was born to be, and I, for once in my goddamn life, wasn't going to drag her down to my level.

"Please, Jordan," Dad whispered. "Let me tell them what happened," he choked out in a pained voice as if the thought disgusted him. *It disgusted me.* "We can help you. You don't have to leave."

"No," I said deadpan. "You gave me your word you wouldn't tell a soul."

"Did you take your meds?" Dad asked after a long pause, changing the subject. "You feeling any better?"

I closed my eyes briefly and counted to ten. As if he even fucking cared. If he knew the half of what I'd been through because of his precious fucking Camryn, he'd shoot himself.

God knows I'd wanted to do it to myself enough times.

"Jordan," Dad said softly. "I know how you're feeling."

You don't have a fucking clue. "I'm sure you do," was my response and it was forced and layered with sarcasm.

"I've been through a breakdown." Dad glanced nervously at my wrists and then at the windshield. "I love you, buddy, and I will do whatever it takes to make this better."

Liar. "Thanks." I pulled the sleeves of my shirt down to cover my scars and inhaled a calming breath.

"Well, I promised I'd get you here," Dad muttered, as he killed the engine and sat back in his seat. "But I still think you should reconsider."

I stared out the passenger window of the car and said, "This won't take long." Inhaling deeply, I focused on the top floor window of the house where the curtains were moving. My heart rate spiked and I felt lightheaded.

Unbuckling my belt, I climbed out of the car and reluctantly made my way up the porch steps with my father by my side, carrying a goddamn pizza.

When we reached the doorway, Dad walked straight into the house, but I took a moment to calm my nerves and force back my guilt.

I was doing the right thing here.

I had to do this.

Hope deserved a man who could give her more. I *couldn't.* I was too fucking damaged and screwed up beyond repair. Love wasn't enough in this instance. Me loving her wasn't enough to erase the pain and her loving me couldn't fix my broken pieces. I was too fucking damaged: therefore I needed to set her free.

"Jordan," Lee said in a soft tone, meeting me in the hallway. "I'm so glad you could come," she told me before wrapping her arms around me. "How's your mom?"

"Thanks for having me, Mrs. Carter. And Mom's doing better," I added softly, stepping back from Hope's mother, feeling furious that Dad had obviously let something slip about what happened in Idaho ... "Uncle Danny is keeping an eye on her until she gets back on her feet."

"That's good." Lee smiled up at me. "I hope things get better for her. For *all* of you."

"Yeah." I nodded stiffly. "Me, too."

"Jordan," Lee said in a coaxing tone. "Are you ... is everything okay?"

"I ..."

I paused and pinched the bridge of my nose. I wanted to tell her, but I couldn't get the damn words out. Clenching my eyes shut, I exhaled heavily. "Is she here?" Opening my eyes again, I looked down at Lee and whispered, "Is she okay?"

"She's upstairs." Kyle's deep voice came from the kitchen doorway. Wrapping an arm around his wife's waist, Kyle pulled her to his side, never taking his eyes off my face. "You can go up," he added.

"Thanks, Mr. Carter," I acknowledged quietly before heading for the staircase.

"Don't hurt her," Kyle called after me. "And I won't hurt you. You got it?"

"Never planned on it."

Breaking it off with Hope was my way of making sure of that.

When I reached her bedroom door, I didn't bother knocking. She knew I was here. Instead I slipped into the room and closed the door behind me. Taking a deep breath and turned around.

When my eyes locked on Hope's face, the pain that hit me directly in the chest was like nothing I'd ever experienced in my life. It was fucking excruciating and knowing what I was about do made it a million times worse.

Sitting cross-legged on her bed, Hope kept her big blue eyes on me as she said, "Care to explain that text message?"

And it was in that moment I realized this would be the hardest fucking thing I would ever do – walking away from that girl – walking away from my Hope.

But she could *never* know.

I'd rather peel my skin off than confess the truth.

Bracing myself for the pain I knew was about to

impale my heart, I allowed the anger that was festering inside of my body take over.

Focusing everything on the fucking shame and disgust inside of me, I glared at the only girl I would ever love and lied through my goddamn teeth ...

"It's over, Hope. I don't want you anymore. This was one huge mistake."

HOPE

Age 18

"It's over, Hope. I don't want you anymore. This was one huge mistake ..."

My brows furrowed as I tried to contemplate what the fuck Jordan had just said to me. "Are you serious ... I mean seriously?"

Jordan remained with his back to my bedroom door, and for the first time in my life, he looked like a complete stranger to me.

Nodding stiffly, he said in a cold tone, "I'm serious."

I exhaled heavily – every ounce of air left my body – and my lungs felt like they had been set on fire. Pain coursed through me. I couldn't speak. I could only shake my head and gape in horror.

"Something happened in Idaho when you went to collect your mother, didn't it?" I blurted out, my brain suddenly clicking into gear. "With your mom?"

When he didn't answer I said, "With Paul?"

Jordan's nostrils flared, his face turned red, and for the first time in my life I was afraid of him.

"I'm not your father, Hope," Jordan sneered as he moved away from the door and strode towards me. "That perfect love?" He leaned forward, getting in my face. "You won't get that from me."

"What are you talking about?" I sobbed, feeling incensed and fucking gutted. "Why are you behaving like this?"

"Because I'm not the person you think I am," Jordan all but roared in my face. "It's over, Hope. We're done, okay? Don't push for more. You don't want to know the truth."

"I do," I shot back angrily, as my temper flared. "Tell me. Give me a goddamn explanation for why you're behaving like this?"

Jordan remained silent and that's when I lost it.

"Fine," I screamed. "Suit yourself, Jordan," I cried. "Ruin your whole life! Wreck mine! Be the fucking asshole that's deep inside you."

Grabbing my neck, Jordan dragged me forwards and plunged his lips to mine. The second his mouth touched mine, I lost a little of myself, but I soon found my senses.

Pushing him roughly away, I raised my hand and slapped him across his face. My hand stung, but I refused to show weakness.

"Don't ever touch me again," I spat, furious. "You think you can put that mouth on me? After what you just said?"

I shook my head in despair and blinked back the tears that were filling my eyes. "Give me something," I croaked out, staring up at the only boy I had ever loved. "This isn't you. Tell me. Tell me!"

Every inch of his body shook as he now blocked me out, pushed me away "I don't love you, Hope," he hissed, jabbing his finger in my face. "Happy now? You were a fucking mistake and I want out."

Lowering his head, Jordan Porter looked me directly in the eyes and said: "I. Don't. Want. *You*."

I stood, frozen to the spot, my heart shattering in my chest as Jordan removed a folded brown envelope from his pocket and tossed it on the floor at my feet before leaving my room.

When I realized what that envelope held, the

broken pieces of my heart turned to stone, my legs gave way beneath me and I crumpled to the floor.

Well, that just showed me …

Jordan Porter had never loved me. *Oh, God!* What was I going to do? I could barely breathe …

Suck it up, Carter!

Suck it up now …

Had he no shame – no soul or heart or anything inside his chest?

Well, I knew the truth now and I would *not* love him. If it killed me, I would *not* love that man again.

It stopped now!

Pressing that crinkled envelope against my chest, I promised myself that I would never let someone do this to me again.

I would never let another man do this to me. *Never again*! No way! I wouldn't let anyone get close enough to hurt me. I would build a wall so damn high around my heart no one would *ever* penetrate it.

JORDAN

Age 21

"Jordan, are you okay?" Logan asked the second I reached the bottom step of the staircase.

Shaking my head, I grabbed my jacket off the banister and shrugged it on quickly. "Tell your sister I'm sorry," I muttered as I opened the front door.

I was close to freedom.

I could almost taste it – if I could just keep my feet moving and my mind blank.

I was almost there ...

Stepping outside, I inhaled a deep breath and forced my legs to move. I was doing the right thing. I knew I was.

I felt someone grab my shoulder and my whole

body shook violently. Every muscle in my body stiffened. I clenched my eyes shut and willed myself to calm down.

"Tell her yourself," Logan said quietly, removing his hand from my arm. "She deserves your words, Jordan," he said. "Not mine."

"My words aren't worth a damn, Low," I growled as I continued down the path towards my father's car.

Jerking the car door open, I swung around to look at the kid who had grown up so much in the past few years he was barely recognizable anymore. "Tell Hope that I'm sorry and just ... just take care of her for me, okay?"

"You're making a mistake," Logan called out, folding his arms across his chest. The wisest of the four Carter kids faced me with an expression of sadness etched on his face. "And you're wrong," Logan added. "Your words are the only words Hope wants – the only ones she'll hear."

"Take care of her."

Climbing into the driver's seat, I slammed the door shut before I could change my mind. I was doing the right thing for the both of us. Time would confirm this. And distance would keep her safe.

II

THE PRESENT

"You've done it again!"

"I have no idea what you're talking about," I lied in an even tone, without breaking my stride. I was in the process of wrapping up my latest book, my word count was at 79,989, and anyone who had ever gotten that far into a story knew just hard those eleven little words could be to find. But knowing I would have to address the matter at hand, I breathed deeply, placed my hands on my lap, and leaned back in my chair.

My roommate, Teagan Connolly, stood in the doorway of my bedroom/office with her hands on her hips and her blonde hair splaying out in forty different directions.

"I've read ten chapters, Hope," she told me. "And Jordan's name is replacing the hero in *every single one*." She was holding a stack of stapled sheets of white paper in one hand and a highlighting pen in the other. She sighed as she added, "Hope, it has been seven years – almost a bloody decade – and you're still moping around the place like a pigeon shat on your head."

"One word, Teegs," I shot back calmly, using my shoeless foot to twist my chair from side to side. *"Noah."*

Teagan couldn't talk.

She was in love with my Uncle Noah.

Yeah, it still felt incredibly weird calling him that, but there it was. Back when we were in high school, Noah's mom revealed he was my father's kid brother. Besides, I knew all about the smutty stack of MMA magazines under my friend's bed with he-who-shall-not-be-named's face etched all over the covers.

Teagan's face contorted in pain and I felt like a bitch for my actions.

"I'm going to pretend you didn't just say his name in my presence," she told me in a shaky voice before slamming the stack of paper and the pen down on my desk. I noticed that her lip was quivering. "Your mom called again," she added. "She wants to know if you got anything *unusual* in the mail."

"No," I lied, shoving the invitation further underneath my keyboard. "Nothing new."

"Hope, I know about your parents' anniversary party tomorrow night – I got an invite, too."

Stopping at the door, Teagan turned around and smiled sadly. "Lee knows you're still hurting over him. She wants to help you, Hope. Maybe you should talk to her about how you're feeling. *Call the woman back.*"

I couldn't talk to anyone about how I was feeling – not vocally at least. The only productive way I seemed to be able to get my pain out was on paper: letting the words spill out and creep across the blank page. Yeah, the page was my canvas and the words were my art. My pen was my paintbrush, and my pain was my story.

I knew I wasn't behaving like a normal twenty-five-year-old woman. I got that. But I couldn't.

Not when I'd had my heart ripped out of my chest at eighteen.

The pain Jordan Porter had put me through had caused a rippling effect on my life. Some days I could barely breathe past it, it hurt so badly. It felt like I'd been knifed through my breastbone and the perpetrator had left the blade inside of my body, forcing me to suffer the agony of breathing in and out with something foreign lodged in my chest.

But I guess that's what love consisted of: having a foreign substance invade your heart.

I missed home, my parents and my siblings, but I couldn't face returning to The Hill. I didn't think I ever could.

I had watched Jordan Porter walk away from me and that annihilation of my trust had damaged my heart beyond all repair. The pain almost killed me on a daily basis. The not knowing where his head was at, or if anything we'd been through had truly been real for him. It cut me deeper than anything else in my entire existence had could or would ...

"I don't love you, Hope. Happy now? You were a fucking mistake and I want out. I. Don't. Want. You."

"I know you think I shouldn't still think about him," I whispered. "*I* know I shouldn't."

Throwing my head back, I covered my face with my hands and fought back the urge to scream. "It just won't fade, Teegs. He's in my head constantly and I hate it."

"You're preaching to the converted here, Hope," Teagan replied with a heavy sigh and I knew that if anyone in the world knew how I was feeling it was Teagan Connolly. "Just do what I do and remind yourself that you didn't do anything wrong," she told me. "Jordan – like *he-who-shall-not-be-named* – happens to be a man: and therefore a stupid, heinous, inconsiderate bastard. I'm telling you, Hope, they're all the same …" Her voice trailed off as she looked at the watch on her wrist in despair. "I'm late for work – we'll finish the man-bitching session when I get home, 'kay?" With that, Teagan turned on her heels and disappeared out of sight.

Sighing guiltily, I pulled myself out of my chair and padded over to my bed. Throwing myself down on the mattress, I tugged my cell phone out of my jeans pocket and dialed my mother's number.

Mom answered on the second ring.

"Hope. Oh, thank God you've called, I was getting worried. Did you get the invitation? When I didn't hear back from you I started to get worried. You know it's tomorrow night, right?"

The obvious relief in my mother's voice made me feel like the world's biggest tool. She didn't need any more worry in her life.

"Hi, Mom," I choked out. "Sorry I haven't called lately. Yeah, I got the invite ..."

"Have you been eating? What about your clothes – can you manage the laundry? You know you can come home anytime you want, in fact I could ..."

"Mom," I said wearily, cutting her off before she had the chance to over-analyze every damn thing in my life. "Yes, I'm doing my laundry." I sniffed the hem of my old *1D* shirt and cringed. "And of course I'm eating." The half-eaten packet of Oreos lying on my bed was proof of that. "Really I'm fine, Mom. How's Dad?" *That ought to work.*

Bringing my father into conversation was a sure way to distract my mother from her examination. Mom and Dad, who were both in their forties, were sickeningly in love. It was truly depressing to me, their daughter, who'd yet to have a serious relationship, yet alone a loving one. They'd gotten together when Mom was a teenager and twenty-six years later they were still going strong; which was great for them, not so much for their kids who had to witness their bubble of love.

Ugh ...

"Wonderful." Mom sighed dreamily, and I wanted to puke. "Working all the hours God gave him as usual. The hotel hasn't been this busy in years."

"That's great," I said honestly. My dad, *Kyle Carter*, inherited a whole bunch of hotels from my great-grandpa before I was born, but lost everything before my first birthday.

My earliest memories of my father were of him working in our backyard, building birdhouses, doghouses and garden fences with Uncle Derek for extra cash. We had been dirt poor until my father won back the hotels when I was eleven.

He was my hero.

His strength was something I would always envy and be in awe of.

"So," Mom said in her soft southern drawl. "Are you excited about coming home this weekend?"

"Sure," I lied. Truth was I couldn't stand the thought of going home. Don't get me wrong, I love my parents deeply, they were loving and supportive, but my family was a little full on.

Our home was usually full of drama and testos-terone-fueled noise.

It was exhausting and I still pinched myself, seven years later, when I woke up in our small apart-ment in peace and isolated calm.

"How are the boys doing?" I asked, smirking to myself, thinking this was another topic I could use to distract my mother. "Causing hell?" *As usual...*

"That's the understatement of the century," she groaned, and I cackled into my pillow. "They're breaking my heart daily," Mom added. "That's why I need my baby girl to come home to me."

Hit me with the mommy card ...

"I'm really busy at the moment, Mom." I knew why she wanted me to come home so badly. I knew what was coming up and I knew exactly *who* would be there. "I'm not sure if I'll be able to come home ..."

"Hope Sarah Carter," my mother said in her *stern* voice. I smiled thinking about my mother being stern. She was about as stern as tissue paper and as aggressive as a goldfish. "You have to come home." She sighed heavily, and I cringed in shame. "It's our twenty-fifth wedding anniversary. Please, sweetie."

God ...

"Is he going to be there?" I asked quietly.

I knew Mom would feel sorry for me, but I didn't care about that.

I needed to know.

There was no way I was putting myself in *that* situation again.

"No," Mom replied after a pause. "I suppose he's feeling the same way you are."

I doubt it.

"Fine," I sighed. "I'll book a flight as soon as you

hang up." I needed to be done with this conversation. I was not dealing with thoughts of *him* today. I couldn't. I would either cry or break my phone. Neither option appealed to me; therefore I was getting off this phone before I lost my choice.

"Hope," Mom said softly, in that tone mothers use when they feel sorry for you, but don't want to come right out and say it. "It has been seven years, sweetheart. Don't you think that it's time you try to move on and forgive him?"

"Could you?" I shot back immediately. "If you were me and *he* was Dad, could you try and move on? Could you *forgive* him?"

I knew the answer to that.

Years ago, when my father had been stabbed by some psychotic freak, my mother had sold everything we owned in order to keep him alive on a feeding tube. He'd been given no hope, laid in a coma for more than half a year and still Mom hadn't given up on him.

According to an old journal of my Aunt Cam's, Dad had treated Mom like shit when they were younger.

Repeatedly.

And she'd forgiven him.

Repeatedly.

Well, I wasn't my mother, and I wasn't going to be any man's doormat.

"Hope, he was young and confused."

"I don't care." I did care. I cared too much. That was the whole freaking problem. "I'm done with this conversation, Mom. I need to finish some work. I'll call you later."

"I need you home," Mom said sadly. "Please. Do this for me."

"One night," I whispered. "And then I'm gone."

"Promise me you'll be there, Hopey-bear?" my mother asked and I found myself nodding reluctantly.

"Yes," I said with a sigh. "I promise."

"Good," Mom chuckled before letting out a worrying sigh. "Please don't blame me for your house guest. That was your father's idea ..."

House guest?

"Mom, what the heck are you talking about ..." I demanded, but the tone on the other end of the line told me that my mother had hung up on me. Then my phone beeped once, signaling I'd received a text message.

Reluctantly I opened it and groaned ...

*   *You wouldn't happen to have a spare bed/couch/bathtub going for your favorite brother?* *

"Damn that man," I screamed, shoving off my covers and leaping out of bed, suddenly understanding my mother's plea. I immediately regretted my tantrum when I noticed the few precious remaining Oreos scatter on the floor.

Diving to where one was rolling under my locker, I wasn't ashamed to say I rubbed if off with my sleeve and took a vicious bite of it.

I needed it.

With my mouth full of chocolate goodness I stalked through our apartment – which consisted of walking from my bedroom through to my kitchen/lounge – and pressed my finger on the buzzer.

"Well if it isn't Dad's favorite minion," I snapped. "How much did he pay you to come here?"

"Not nearly enough," I heard Colton chuckle. "Buzz me in. I'm freezing. You can chew me out in person in the *warmth*."

"Fine," I muttered, buzzing him and opening my apartment door. "It's open."

I went and grabbed a hair tie from our poky bathroom and rearranged my hair into a messy half-bun/half-ponytail before grabbing a carton of orange juice from the fridge.

Teagan and I badly needed to clean the place up, but Colton was a bigger slob than both of us combined, so I doubted he would notice my crap.

"Love what you've done with the place," I heard my brother say, and I mentally braced myself before turning around.

"The mold is a fascinating addition," Colt chuckled, signaling to a pile of dirty laundry in my overflowing hamper. "And the smell." He grinned and clicked his tongue. "Very new age, Hopey-bear."

"Don't call me that." I shuddered, glaring at the big ape that was making himself comfortable on my couch. "How long are you here for?"

"Depends," Colt replied, casually folding his arms behind his head. "Board that plane with me in fifteen hours and I'll be out of your hair in a jiffy. Or *don't* and I stay and annoy you until you give in and come home." He twisted his neck from side to side and grinned at me. "Feel free to stay, I could do with a challenge. I'm getting bored with my life."

"You're getting bored with your life?" I rolled my eyes and sighed. "Colt, you're twenty-three. What could possibly be boring about your life? This is Dad's doing, right?"

Colton shrugged. "Dad wanted a solid guarantee you would be in that hotel tomorrow night." Smirking, he added, "Mom is worried about you. Dad is worried about Mom. Mom wants you at the party, and Dad wants to put a smile on Mom's face. I just happen to be the messenger boy."

With my shoulders slumped, I trudged over to the couch and plopped down, feeling weirdly comforted with having my brother so close after so long apart. "I gather Dad's still a huge control freak," I grumbled. "This sucks."

"I'm going to pretend you didn't just say that," Colt mused. "Look, Hope, I know Jordan-the-douchebag-Porter did something pretty damn bad to chase you half way across the world, but don't let him be the cause of breaking Mom's heart."

"I didn't leave *because* of him," I shot back defensively, lying through my teeth.

"Maybe so," Colt replied calmly. Sitting up, he wrapped his arm around my shoulder and pulled me close to him. "But you haven't come home because of *him*. I have no idea what happened between you two, Hope," he said quietly and in a weirdly serious tone. "Neither does Cam, or Low, but you are *our* sister, and we've got your back."

"Thank you," I whispered, but I was shaking

inside. My nerves were frazzled and the prospect of seeing that man again was causing my anxiety to rise to epic proportions.

"So," Colt said, clearing his throat. "We've got about fifteen hours to waste until our flight. Do wanna go get drunk?"

"Yeah, Colt," I said with a sigh. "I really do."

HOPE

The heat inside Krash nightclub was almost unbearable.

I had only ever been here once before, it was damn close to impossible to gain admission, but my congenial brother had charmed his – and my way – through the shiny black doors to where I was currently occupying a barstool in the exclusive private area of the club.

I wasn't a fan of nightclubs. I wasn't a fan of being crushed by sweaty, overbearing men and braless bimbos either. Men prowled the bar looking for alcohol and release, but I was here for one reason and one reason only: to drown my sorrows and forget about my impending doom.

That was it.

Swallowing what had to be my tenth shot of *Jameson*, I brushed the hand that had landed on my shoulder roughly away and gazed around the room through bleary eyes.

I spotted Colton on the dance floor, surrounded by a group of women, and snorted loudly. One voluptuous blonde was clinging to Colton like he was her chosen mate. Another skinny brunette was grinding against his broad back. Their bodies rubbed against my baby brother, sweat slickened, and I had to swallow some vomit before turning my face away from the sight.

The atmosphere in the private area was energetic – there seemed to be a dynamic buzz in the air. There was a group of girls literally screaming and pointing at the booth furthest away from where I was sitting, and that caught my attention.

When I realized exactly *who* those girls were pointing at, my stomach fell into my ass.

I watched in drunken horror as an insanely attractive man covered in tattoos stood up and tossed back a shot before moving through the crowd of women towards the bar – towards me.

His gaze locked on my face and instant recognition flared in his brown eyes.

"Hope."

Oh crapola ...

Jerking off my stool, I pushed past several people, desperate to get away from my uncle, but he moved faster, shoving people out of his way in his bid to reach me.

"Is she here?" he roared. "Is Teagan with you?"

"Stay away from her, Noah," I slurred, as I stumbled down the staircase towards the exit.

I needed to get home and warn Teagan her worst nightmare was partying in a club ten minutes from our apartment.

Shit.

―――――――

"Hope, I swear to God I am going to tie your key around your bloody…"

Teagan's voice trailed off the moment she opened the door and caught a glimpse of my face.

"What's wrong?"

"He's here, Teagan," I choked out as I barreled into her arms. "In Cork. I saw him – at the club," I added. "He's *here*."

"Who?" Teagan demanded. "Who's here, Hope?"

"Noah," I hissed, and then quickly clapped my

hand over my mouth. "He saw me," I added. "Teagan, he knows you're here."

"What?" Teagan's voice was small and frightened. Her face was pale and her brown eyes wide as saucers. "What did you say?"

Pushing us both into the room, I swung around and slammed the apartment door before bolting it. With my back pressed to the door, I let out a huge sigh of relief. "There," I half-slurred, half-hiccuped. "That'll keep the big douche out."

"A deadbolt?" Shaking her head, Teagan clawed at her hair as she looked around frantically. "You really think a fucking deadbolt is going to keep *him* out ..."

"Hope!"

I heard my name being roared out seconds before the sound of banging infiltrated my eardrums and a hard vibration penetrated my back.

"Face him, Teegs," I told her. "Just get it over and done with."

"Like you faced Jordan?" she shot back, nostrils flaring. "Hmm?"

Okay, fuck it! Live like me. Be a goddamn coward.

"Jesus Christ," Teagan whispered, before rushing over to help me barricade the door with her body.

"Hope, I know you're in there. Open the goddamn door, or I'll kick it in."

"Go away, you big ass," I screeched, stumbling away from the door.

"Hide," I mouthed to Teagan and she did.

Running like headless chickens through our own pokey apartment, Teagan dove behind the couch and I crouched behind the coffee table just as the door of our apartment was smashed clean off its hinges.

I peeked up from my hiding spot to see Noah Messina standing in the doorway of our apartment, looking more furious than I had ever seen him look.

"Is that any way to speak to your uncle?" Noah's voice was calm, but the way his fists were clenched and trembling at his sides assured me he was anything but. His dark eyes were focused entirely on my roommate as he ran a hand through his thick black hair.

"Thorn."

I opened my mouth to respond, but Teagan spoke before I had a chance.

"How dare you come in here," she screamed before somersaulting over the back of our couch and launching herself at my uncle.

"Hear me out."

"Go to hell."

"I've been there, sweetheart, and it's not fucking pretty."

I felt incredibly lightheaded as I watched my father's kid brother wrestle my brazen best friend into submission. "You're believing a lie, Thorn," Noah snapped, as he pressed Teagan against the wall. *"Dammit, stop fucking biting me!"*

"I loved you," I heard Teagan whisper, almost begrudgingly, and my heart broke for her. "I *loved* you, Noah."

But I didn't hear Noah's response, as the alcohol in my veins and the exhaustion in my heart dragged me under.

HOPE

From the age of eighteen I had a plan – leave Colorado and never return.

Up until twenty-four hours ago my plan had been unfolding beautifully. The space I had managed to put between my past mistakes – Jordan – and the person I was now, had saved my life and sparked to life a career in writing that I wasn't sure I would have pursued had I remained in Colorado.

Yet, one phone call from my mother had brought me back there, standing in the middle of the airport to be exact, almost choking to death on all my past mistakes. After thirteen long hours of traveling with the hangover from *hell*, I finally set foot on Colorado soil again, and every memory I'd forced to the back of my mind impaled my heart.

Lowering my sunglasses to cover my red-rimmed eyes, I inhaled deeply, collected my suitcase from luggage, and, with my worse-for-wear brother in tow, headed outside to the drop off area.

Colton and I both looked like shit, having slept less than three hours between us, but at least we were together.

"Not so fast," Colt grumbled, as he wobbled beside me. "The ground is still spinning."

"That would be the Jaeger Bombs," I chuckled, as I walked through the revolving glass doors of the airport. "You'll survive."

"I might," Colt agreed, grabbing my arm quickly in a bid to stay upright. "But I can't say the same for Teagan. Noah looked mad as hell when I swung by to pick you up …"

"I'm too hung over to worry about those two, Colt." I wrapped my arm around his shoulder to stop him from falling on his ass.

Baby brother was a lightweight …

"*Do a shot, Colton,*" he groused, as he attempted to steady himself. "It'll be *fine*, Colton. You forgot to warn me about the possibility of losing my fucking balance."

The retort I was about to make died on the tip of my tongue as my eyes locked on the shiny, black

Range Rover pulling up on the curb in front of us. The driver's door flew open and a pair of piercing blue eyes greeted me.

"Angel."

My face broke out in a huge smile the second my eyes fastened on my father, leaning against the hood of his car, dressed in a finely-cut black suit, with his arms folded across his chest and his head tilted to one side.

I hadn't realized I'd missed him so much.

I couldn't help myself. I squealed "Daddy," and ran towards him. He caught me easily and enveloped me in one of those *nothing-can-harm-me-he's-got-me* hugs.

"Jesus, I've missed you," Dad husked, setting me back on my feet. He locked his blindingly-blue eyes on my face. "You doing okay?"

"Everything's fine," I said, patting his shoulder. "Well, apart from the douche you sent me."

"*Daddy*," Colt cried out in a mocking tone, shoving me out of the way and grabbing our father in a bear hug. "I've missed you *so* much."

Dad laughed, and I was sure he enjoyed Colt's playful nature. "We've talked about this, Colt," Dad taunted. "Five second delay."

"Have we time to go home and change before

going to the hotel?" I asked my father when we were sitting in his truck on the way back towards The Hill. I was dressed in jeans and a hoodie – hardly formal party attire.

Dad took a quick glance at his wristwatch before letting out a sigh.

"You got a dress in your case?" he asked, as he ran a hand through his thick dark hair and used the other to steer, eyes locked on the windshield.

"Yeah," I started to say. "But …"

"Then you can get dressed in one of the suites at the hotel," Dad replied. "Your mother will have my balls if I don't get you there on time," he added in a petulant tone, before pulling at his tie. "That woman can be bossy as hell when she wants to be."

"Sure she can," I responded dryly, barely refraining from rolling my eyes to heaven.

JORDAN

"Are you excited to see your family tonight?" Annabelle asked me and I smiled.

I smiled and lied through my teeth.

"Sure I am," I told her, pressing a kiss to her brow.

Coming back here was a mistake. I knew it. I just couldn't do a damn thing to change it. My hands were tied, damn it.

Every instinct in my body was demanding I get the hell out of this place – to fucking run.

But I had been running for seven years and being on the road was tiring.

Besides, I owed this to Lee.

I just had to suck it up and make it through the next three hours.

HOPE

He was here.

With a woman.

He came to my parents' anniversary party with a fucking woman.

A beautiful woman.

I couldn't breathe.

I didn't want to.

The tension in the room was palpable and I had to admit the only reason I wasn't running for the hills was because of the six-inch stilettos on my feet and the firm hold Colton had on my arm.

"Ignore him," Colt whispered gently, guiding me further away from the *pair*. "She's barely a three."

I closed my eyes and fought back my tears, allowing my brother to lead me away. "A three?"

"Yeah, and that's out of one hundred." Colton sighed heavily and threw his arm over my shoulder, tucking me under his arm. "Don't sweat it, Hope, you've got the edge on her plastic ass."

"Gee, thanks," I muttered, allowing Colton to lead me over to where our other brothers were lounging near the bar, surrounded by a flock of beautiful women.

I was tall for a woman at 5'9", but my brothers were huge. Clocking in at 6'2", all three boys towered over me. We all shared the same dark hair and blue eyes, except for Logan, who got Mom's gray eyes.

"Well, look what the horse dragged in," Cam mused.

Colt was the horse; I was the 'what'.

"Looking like shit, sis," Cam said with a smirk. "And wider," he added.

I merely raised my middle finger at Cam in response, but my stupid damn eyes kept filling with tears.

"What the fuck, Cam," Logan said in a weary tone. "Put a filter on it, douchebag."

Cam sobered his features quickly when he noticed my tears, and jumped off the bar stool he was sitting on.

"You're not wide," he rambled, clearly flustered. "You're skinny. I'm wide. And stupid. You know I didn't mean that. I was talking shit … you know I have a problem with my mouth. Shit, I'm an asshole," he said, stopping in front of me.

"Jesus, Hope," Cameron groaned, lifting my chin with his hand. "Don't waste your tears on an asshole like me."

In a rare act of tenderness, Cameron pulled me into his arms and squeezed me tightly. "Be sure that the man who makes you cry is worth the pain," he said quietly. "I'm not."

"She's not crying over you," Logan hissed as he flanked me, his eyes locked on the opposite side of the room. "Our sister is crying because of that ignorant piece of shit over there groping that mediocre-looking blonde."

"I'll fucking kill him," Cam snarled, before turning on his heel and storming off in the direction of my worst nightmare.

With my shoulders slumped, I trudged over to barstool Cam had vacated and hoisted myself onto it, watching in horror as my brother stalked across the foyer towards where Jordan was mingling.

"I see he's still as bad-tempered," I grumbled,

watching Cameron having a heated discussion with Jordan across the room. "What an idiot."

Colt stared at me like I'd grown an extra head. "Cam's trying to defend you," he said slowly.

"He needs to feel like he's doing something," Logan interrupted calmly, leaning against the bar beside me. "You know how Cam gets."

Shaking his head, Logan ran his hand through his thick dark hair and exhaled slowly. "Things have been … hard for Cameron," he said quietly and in a weirdly serious tone. "Shit's been going down like you wouldn't believe."

"Low," Colt snapped, clearing his throat, eyes locked on Logan. "Are you gonna stop him or am I?"

"Give him a few minutes," Logan replied calmly, nodding towards where Jordan and Cameron were most definitely having words. "He needs the release."

"I need to get out of here," I told my brothers. This was all too much for me. Hell, I should have never come back for this stupid party.

Climbing off the barstool, I pushed my way through the throngs of people celebrating my parents' relationship and I could have cried out in relief when I reached the elevators.

"Hope."

The deep gravelly timbre of his voice shook my

resolve. I had to force down the emotions that came from hearing that name on his lips.

"Jordan," I acknowledged, as I continued pressing the button on the wall beside the elevator. Thankfully, the doors slid open and I hurried inside.

The strong hand that clamped my arm halted my escape and shook me to my very core.

"Let go," I said in a quiet, but no-nonsense tone of voice. My teeth were threatening to chatter so I bit down hard on my lips and tried to tug my arm free.

"Now."

Jordan didn't let go. Instead, he stepped into the elevator, the scent of him overpowering me, making me drunk. "Give me five minutes," he said, as he the elevator doors closed, trapping me inside with the man who broke my goddamn heart. "And then I'll let you go."

"You let me go years ago," I shot back stiffly, pulling free, my hackles standing. The elevator descended quickly, causing my stomach to flip. "But I'll hear you out."

"Not here," was all Jordan said, and the next thing I knew the elevator doors had opened and I was being dragged through the basement floor of my father's hotel. Of course, I didn't need to ask Jordan where we were going. I already knew.

The pool.

"This must be a new thing for you," I said cattily, as Jordan switched on the lights in the pool room and gestured me in. "Having to force a girl to go somewhere with you."

"I didn't force you, Hope," he replied quietly from behind me – too close behind me. "And this was long overdue."

"I'm not interested in hearing what you have to say," I shot back, as I stood at the edge of the pool, looking down at the stillness of the water.

Sitting down on the floor, I removed my sandals before sinking my toes into the water, feeling desperately drawn to Jordan as always. I knew he was bad for me, the bastard basically broke me seven years ago, but I sure as hell was a glutton for punishment because a part of me *wanted* to be here with him … How messed up was that?

"I know you're not interested," I heard Jordan say. His footsteps echoed to my left moments before he sat next to me.

"And I know why. I'm sorry."

"Fine," I replied coldly. "You're sorry. Good for you. Is that it?"

"Is it not enough?" he asked softly.

Damn it, I could never understand what he was

thinking – what he meant with these short sentences.

"Who's the girl?" I said, mentally cringing, and feeling furious with myself for asking the one question I'd swore I wouldn't ask him.

"Her name's Annabelle," he replied. "She's my girlfriend," he added after a long pause.

Ouch ... cut me fucking to the bone.

"That's nice," I managed to say, though I had no idea how. "Annabelle and Jordan. *Cute.*"

Jordan flinched. "Don't, Keychain."

"When's the wedding?" I snapped. "Sure looked like a dazzler of a ring on her finger."

"It's not …" He stopped, pinched the bridge of his nose, and shrugged his shoulders.

"I need to cool down."

Standing up, he peeled off his dress shirt and pants, kicked off his shoes and socks before diving into the pool.

I remained frozen, riveted to the spot, as I watched him flex muscles on his body as he swam to the surface that hadn't been there seven years ago.

"May," he said finally, as he pushed his wet hair off his face and waded towards me. "The tenth."

Son of a bitch ...

He looked at me apologetically as if he knew it

would upset me to find out he was planning to get married on my birthday.

"Next year," he added quietly.

Rub salt in my wounds, asshole ...

"Huh," I growled in a fake-as-fuck voice.

Pulling myself to my feet, I glared down at him.

"Getting married on my birthday. That's pretty tasteless, Jordan," I said, my voice laced with anger as I backed away from him, before turning around and stalking off towards the door.

I heard the sound of water splashing seconds before the words, "I'm sorry," penetrated my eardrums.

"You should be," I hissed, swinging around to face him. Jordan was already staring down at me, his green eyes locked on my face.

"I suppose I should leave my forwarding address with you."

Jordan stared blankly at me, and I shook my head in disgust. "You know, for my invitation," I told him sweetly. "Oh, and the divorce papers you'll need me to sign."

Jordan paled, and I swallowed the huge lump in my throat.

"The annulment papers," he said slowly. "I signed them. You were supposed to ..."

"Our marriage was *consummated*, Jordan," I spat, interrupting his denial, hurting all over to think being married to me made him feel so sick. "If you want a new Mrs. Porter, you're going to have to get rid of the old one first."

HOPE

It was four days later, when I was soaking in my
bathtub back home in Cork, and reading through
my text messages, that I realized I hadn't left a
forwarding address for Jordan. He certainly remembered my phone number, though...

Jordan: We need to talk.

Jordan: Hope, don't ignore me. You
can't drop a bomb like that and run
away.

Jordan: I know I've done some things
that are unforgivable, but we need to

talk about this. If you won't call me, then text me.

Jordan: Hope, it's been three days. I can't sleep. I can't fucking think about anything. I feel like my life's been put on pause. Call me. We need to resolve this.

Jordan: Come on, Keychain. Answer me.

I didn't answer him.

Instead, I chose to let Jordan Porter wallow in his misery. He had so easily forgotten about me back then, so why should I run to him and wag my tail like a dog?

I wouldn't.

It simply wasn't my style. I wasn't the roll-over-and-beg–for-attention type of girl and Jordan Porter could go fuck himself for all I cared.

I was done.

I would sign his stupid papers, but I sure as hell wasn't going to make it easy for him – and *Annabelle*.

I scoffed loudly and laid my head back, allowing the bubbles and water to encase me. God, I loved the bathtub in this place.

I planned on ignoring the asshole hammering on my apartment door, but then I thought of Mrs. Crowley next door. Teagan wasn't home and Mrs. Crowley was frail and elderly. Loud noises terrified the poor woman.

Grumbling to myself, I hauled myself out of the tub, wrapped the only clean towel I had left – a thin, ratty blue one that had seen better days – before trudging out to the kitchen/lounge and opening our shiny new apartment door.

The angry retort I had on the tip of my tongue died the moment my eyes locked on his intense green ones.

"What are you …?" My voice trailed off, my tongue felt like sandpaper, and I licked my lips to moisten them before readjusting my scanty towel.

"Doing here?" Jordan added coldly, never taking his eyes off my face. "What else did you expect me to do?"

Go away …

Leave me alone …

Never contact me again …

All of my silent answers must have shown in my eyes or something because Jordan nodded stiffly and shifted around. "You dropped one hell of a bomb-shell on me, Keychain," he mused.

Dropping a duffel bag on the floor at his feet, he lowered a guitar case to rest at his side. "Are you going to invite me in, or do you want to have this conversation in the hallway – dressed like that?"

"I'm fine here," I shot back, refusing to feel embarrassed. Screw it. I wasn't embarrassed. I was, however, furious, and having Jordan here caused that irritation to soar. "It shouldn't take long."

"Suit yourself," he countered evenly, as his gaze slowly drifted downwards, resting on my barely covered chest. Jordan's eyes darkened, but I refused to cover myself. Let him look. That's all he would be doing. "Where would you like to start?"

"Hmm." I pretended to think about it for a second before raising my hand and smacking his cheek with the palm of my hand. "That's as good a place as any," I replied as my chest heaved. My palm stung, but the relief I felt was huge.

"I deserved that one," Jordan said gruffly, eyes locked on mine.

"No," I hissed. "You deserve two thousand, five hundred and sixty more where that came from – one for every day you've been a complete asshole to me – but I happen to need the use of my hand for work, so you'll have to settle with one."

"You're still my wife," he said eventually.

"Yep," I said sarcastically. "And I'm really sorry, honey, but I forgot to put the pot-roast in the oven. Shall I grab your slippers, or run you a bath instead?"

He glared at me. "Don't joke, Hope."

I glared back at him. "Don't tell me what to do, Jordan."

"I wouldn't dare," he chuckled softly. "You're still as stubborn as ever."

"What can I say," I snapped, clutching the opening of my towel with a death grip. "It's a defense mechanism I got from my mother."

"You get it from your father, Keychain," Jordan mused. "You're nothing like your mom."

"I could say the same about you," I muttered, letting the door swing inwards.

He was right.

This wasn't the kind of conversation I wanted to have in a hallway. I was freezing and Jordan was unsettling me. "And please refrain from calling me that," I added as I turned around and headed straight for my bedroom, not bothering to check and see if he was following.

Jordan could do as he pleased.

Meanwhile, I was layering myself up. I felt too

exposed around him, but I doubted any amount of clothing could change that. He simply had that effect on me.

Grabbing a T-shirt and sweats from my wardrobe, I dressed quickly and went into the bathroom to let the water out of my bath before heading back to the lounge.

Jordan was standing in my lounge. When he saw me his brow creased. "You still have that shirt?"

I looked down at myself and cringed.

Years ago, during my pop music phase, I had forced Jordan to drive eighty miles out of State to a *1D* concert. He had been disgusted with me, but I hadn't cared and had even persuaded him to dance with me that night.

Jordan was an amazing dancer, but you would never be able to tell by the way he kept himself so far apart from the rest of the world. *So unattached and aloof ...*

The pink shirt with the band members' faces was well worn now, but one of my secret comforts. The fact that I'd kept it meant more than I would ever let on. Jordan had already messed me up so badly, I wouldn't let him know it. "It's comfy," was all I replied.

He nodded and remained quiet so I decided to make coffee. Call it a nervous trait, but I couldn't stand awkward silences. I wasn't one of those people who could sit quietly with strangers. I either made conversation or I left. Simple as that. That's that way Jordan seemed to me now and my heart hurt with that truth.

I had spent years of my life in his company, glued to his side, but now, standing in my kitchen with him a few feet behind me, I had never felt so disconnected with him … so alone and sad.

I couldn't believe this was what had happened to us after eighteen years of friendship.

It seriously sucked.

"Hope, can you stop moving around and talk to me for a while?"

"I'm thirsty," I replied and continued busying myself with making coffee – anything to delay the inevitable.

"We need to talk," I heard him say. "Hope, we need to sort this out."

"You need to sort this out. I need a drink," I shot back. "That's what I need." I knew why he was here. I knew what he wanted. I just didn't know if I was strong enough to give it to him.

Jordan growled impatiently. "Can you do what you're told," he snapped as he stalked towards me, getting in my personal space. "For once in your goddamn life?"

"Why break the habit of a lifetime?" I snapped, folding my arms across my chest and glaring up at the man in front of me.

Shaking his head, Jordan tutted loudly. "You're such a brat."

"Yeah, well, you're such an asshole," I growled. "What's new?"

Backing me up against the fridge, Jordan stepped closer until his shoes were touching my bare toes. "Spoilt, entitled little daddy's girl," he rasped, and there was a glint of humor in his eyes.

"Overgrown momma's boy," I retorted, as my heart hammered against my chest.

"You're pushing me, Keychain," Jordan husked with a smirk.

An answer was on the tip of my tongue, but it got lost when I noticed the hunger burning in Jordan's green eyes. We were closer than we had been in seven years. "Don't marry her," I blurted out instead.

I didn't blush.

I didn't flinch.

Instead, I stared into his eyes, daringly, forcing him to see me – to see what he was throwing away. "Don't do it," I repeated, holding my breath, fearing his answer. "We have unfinished business and you know it."

"What are you saying?" he whispered.

I didn't know what I was saying. All I was sure about was what I felt in my bones and this man had not been put on this earth for any woman other than me.

"You know what I'm saying," I breathed, chest heaving. "Don't marry her."

Have me ...

Rubbing his jaw with his hand, Jordan sighed heavily. "She's not to blame here, Hope," he whispered. "All she did was fall in love with ..."

"My husband," I snapped. "All she did was fall in love with *my* husband." Folding my arms across my chest, I glared up at me. "Doe she even know about me?" I demanded. "About us?"

"Hope," Jordan pleaded. "You know I'm no good for you." His body trembled as he spoke. "You're young," he added, in an almost desperate tone "You'll do all of this again – with someone else, someone better than me."

"Say you don't love me," I hissed, grabbing the labels of his shirt and dragging him closer. "Look me in the eyes and tell me you don't love me and I'll sign your papers."

To be continued.

THANK YOU SO MUCH FOR
READING!

Hope and Jordan's story continues in
Inevitable, Carter Kids #5
Available now.

Fall on Me – Broken #3

Forever we Fall – Broken #4

Breaking Point – Broken #4.5 (TBR)

The Carter Kids Series:

Treacherous – Carter Kids #1

Always – Carter Kids #1.5

Thorn – Carter Kids #2

Tame – Carter Kids #3

Avenged – Carter Kids #3.5 (TBR)

Torment – Carter Kids #4

Cameron – Carter Kids #4.5 (TBR)

Inevitable – Carter Kids #5

Trust – Carter Kids #5.5 (TBR)

Altered – Carter Kids #6

Addicted – Carter Kids #6.5 (TBR)

The DiMarco Dynasty:

DiMarco's Secret Love Child: Part One

DiMarco's Secret Love Child: Part Two

The Blurred Lines Duet:

Blurring Lines – Book #1

Never Let me Go – Book #2

Boys of Tommen:

Binding 13 – Book #1

Keeping 13 – Book #2

Saving 6 – Book #3 (TBR)

Crellids:

The Bastard Prince

Titles Available as Audiobooks:

Treacherous – Carter Kids #1

Thorn – Carter Kids #2

Tame – Carter Kids #3

Binding 13 – Boys of Tommen #1 (Part One)

Binding 13 – Boys of Tommen #1 (Part Two)

The Pocketful Series – Coming Soon

For more information on audiobooks, please check out Chloe's website <u>here</u>.

The Broken Series and Carter Kids Series reading order:

1. Break my Fall

2. Fall to Pieces

3. Fall on Me

4. Forever we Fall

5. Treacherous

6. Always

7. Thorn

8. Tame

9. Avenged

10. Torment

11. Cameron

12. Inevitable

13. Trust

14. Altered

15. Addicted

16. Breaking Point

The Blurred Lines duo reading order:

1. Blurring Lines

2. Never Let me Go

The DiMarco Dynasty reading order:

1. DiMarco's Secret Love Child: Part One

2. DiMarco's Secret Love Child: Part Two

The Faking It trilogy reading order:

1. Off Limits

2. Off the Cards

3. Off the Hook

Boys of Tommen Series:

1. Binding 13

2. Keeping 13

3. Saving 6

Pocket Series:

1. Pocketful of Blame

2. Pocketful of Shame

3. Pocketful of You

4. Pocketful of Us

International bestselling author Chloe Walsh writes heart wrenching, emotionally gripping, young and new adult fiction. Her books will suck you into deeply emotive storylines, where you'll fall in love with the complex, sexy heroes, hilarious sidekicks, and lovable female leads. Every adventure with Chloe is an angsty plot designed to give you the ultimate book hangover.

Chloe hails from a small town in the beautiful West Cork on the south coast of Ireland, where she resides with her two children and the tall, dark, and handsome man in her life – Garry, her overgrown Newfoundland pup. When Garry isn't dragging her around the farmer's fields and countryside lanes, she can be found glued to her kindle or binging on Netflix, inhaling GOT, devouring all things rugby, drowning in her Spotify playlists, and being a kick-ass autism mommy.

Animal lover, music addict, TV junkie, Chloe is your typical twenty-nine-year-old, with a passion for reading and an even bigger passion for putting pen to paper. A fiercely proud champion of mental health awareness, Chloe makes no secret of her own personal battles and construes this in her writing.

At present, she has more than twenty novels under her belt, many of which are bestsellers in multiple countries around the world. Several of her titles have been turned into audiobooks.

The best way to get in touch with Chloe is in her reader group on Facebook **Chloe's Clovers**.

Join Chloe's mailing list for exclusive content, release updates, and a free eBook:
http://eepurl.com/dPzXM1

To keep up to date with Chloe's upcoming releases, you can follow her on any of the platforms listed below:

Mailing List

Facebook

Reader Group

Twitter

Instagram

Goodreads

BookBub

Spotify

Amazon

Website

Made in the USA
Las Vegas, NV
06 January 2023

65148132R00090